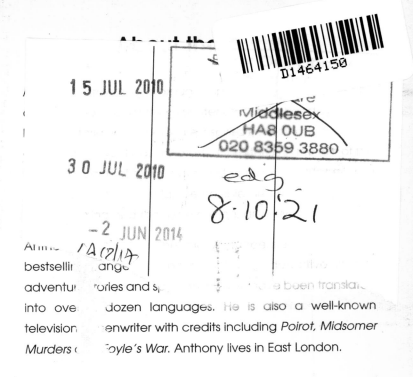

About the

An... /A (?/17

bestselli ange

adventu rories and s... ...e been translate

into ove... dozen languages. He is also a well-known

television enwriter with credits including *Poirot*, *Midsomer*

Murders ... *oyle's War*. Anthony lives in East London.

'A first clas hildren's novelist'
TIMES EDUCATIONAL SUPPLEMENT

'Perfec or readers with an appetite for ghoulish
happen gs'
SCHOO RARIAN ASSOCIATION

'Suspen ..ful and exciting'
BOOKS FOR KEEPS

BURNT

To <u>Silvia</u>, <u>Hen</u>, <u>Ben</u> & Tim.

It was good to see you.

Orchard Books
338 Euston Road, London NW1 3BH
Orchard Books Australia
Hachette Children's Books
Level 17/207 Kent Street, Sydney, NSW 2000

First published by Orchard Books in 1999 or 2000
This edition published in 2008
Text copyright © Anthony Horowitz 1999

A CIP catalogue record for this book is available from the British Library

ISBN 978 1 84616 966 3

1 3 5 7 9 10 8 6 4 2

www.orchardbooks.co.uk

Printed and bound in Great Britain by CPI Bookmarque, Croydon, CR0 4TD

Orchard Books is a division of Hachette Children's Books,
an Hachette Livre UK company.

ANTHONY HOROWITZ

BURNT

ORCHARD BOOKS

Contents

BURNT

July 10th
Three
weeks
in
Barbados.

A smart hotel on the beach. Surfing, sailing and water-skiing. All expenses paid. It sounds like the star prize on a TV game show and I suppose I ought to be over the moon. Or over the Caribbean anyway. But here's the bad news. I'm going with Uncle Nigel and Aunt Sara.

Mum told me this morning. The new baby is due in the middle of August and she's not going anywhere. There's no question of Dad going anywhere without her. He's gone completely baby mad. If he spends any more time in Mothercare they'll probably give him a job there. The point is, if I don't go with Nigel and Sara, I'm not going to get a summer holiday and Mum thinks it would be easier for everyone if I was out of the way. This is what comes of having another baby thirteen years after the last one. The last one, of course, was me.

A NOTE ON SARA HOWARD.

She's quite a bit older than Mum and looks it. Forty-something? She's fighting a battle with old age and I'm afraid she's not on the winning side. Grey hair, glasses, a slightly pinched face. She never smiles very much although Mum says she was a laugh when she was young. She has small, dark eyes that give nothing away. Dad says she's sly. It's certainly true that you can never tell what she's thinking.

She has no children of her own and Mum said she was happy to take me with her to Barbados but I know this is not true. I overheard them talking last night.

SARA: I'm sorry, Susan. I can't take him. The thing is, I have plans.

MUM: But Tim won't get a holiday if you don't help out, Jane. He'll be as good as gold and we'll pay his way...

SARA: It's not a question of money...

MUM: You said you wanted to help.

SARA: I know. But...

And so on. I wondered why she was being so difficult. Maybe she just wanted to be on her own with Uncle Nigel.

A NOTE ON NIGEL HOWARD.

I don't like him. That's the truth. First of all, he's such an awkward, ugly man that I feel embarrassed just being with him. He's tall, thin and bald. He has a round, pale face, no chin but a very long neck. He reminds me of a diseased ostrich. All his clothes came from Marks and Spencer and none of them fit. He's the headmaster of a small private school in Wimbledon and he never lets you forget it. All in all, he has the same effect on me as five fingernails scratching down a blackboard. I wonder why Sara married him?

August 12th

Stayed last night in N & S's house in West London. A Victorian terrace with rising damp. Cases packed and in the hall. We're waiting for the taxi that hasn't arrived. My uncle and aunt had quite an argument about it. He blamed her for not calling the firm that he always uses.

NIGEL: Speedway are much more reliable. Why didn't you call Speedway?

SARA: Because you're always telling me they're too expensive.

NIGEL: For God's sake, woman! How much do you think it's going to cost us if we miss the plane?

Then they argued about the packing. It turns out that Uncle Nigel is absolutely determined to get a sun tan. I wouldn't have said this was possible as he has pale, rather clammy skin that looks as if it's never even seen the sun. Dad once told me that his nickname at the school where he teaches is Porridge...which is, I'm afraid, more or less his colour. Anyway, Nigel wanted to be certain that Sara had packed his sun tan oil and in the end she was forced to open the case and show him.

He had six bottles of the stuff! He had those bottles

that come locked together with different sun protection factors. The higher the factor number, the greater the protection. He had oil to go on first thing in the morning and more oil for last thing at night. He had water-resistant oil, hypo-allergenic oil and UVA-protective oil. But he still wasn't satisfied. 'Have you opened this?' he asked, taking out one of the bottles. 'Of course I haven't opened it, dear,' Sara said. She put the bottle back in the case and closed it up again.

The taxi has just arrived. Uncle Nigel was so angry about how late it was that he smashed a vase in the hall. It was the vase Mum gave to Aunt Sara for her birthday. She's sweeping up the pieces now.

August 15th

Things are looking up.

Barbados is a really ace place. Palm trees everywhere and sea so blue it's dazzling. When you go swimming you see fishes that come in every shape and colour and the night is filled with steel drums and the smell of rum. The beaches go on for ever and it's boiling hot, at least ninety. Our hotel is on the west of the island, near Sandy Lane Bay. It's small and modern but right on the beach and friendly and there are other boys of my age staying here so I'm not going to be on my own.

Anyway, N & S have more or less forgotten me which suits me fine. Sara has spent the last two days beside the pool, under a big sun umbrella, reading the latest Stephen King. Nigel doesn't like Stephen King. He gave us a long lecture over dinner about how horror stories are unhealthy and pander to peoples' basest instincts...whatever that means. Apparently he banned Goosebumps from his school.

He's bagged a sun lounger out on the beach and he spent the whole day out there, lying on his back in his baggy Marks and Spencer swimming trunks. He made Sara rub Factor 15 all over him and I could tell she didn't much enjoy it. Without his clothes on, Nigel manages to be scrawny and plump at the same time. He has no muscles at all and his little pot belly hangs over the waistband of his trunks. He has a thin coating of ginger hair. I suppose he must have been ginger before he went bald. I watched Sara sliding her hands over his chest and shoulders, spreading the oil, and I could see the look on her face. It was as if she was trying not to be sick.

While she read and he sunbathed, I went out with Cassian who's thirteen and who's here with his family for two weeks. They come from Crouch End which isn't too far from where I live. We went swimming and snorkelling. Then we played tennis on the hotel court. Cassian's going to ask his mum and dad if we can hire a jet ski tomorrow but he says they'll probably only pay for a pedalo.

Dinner at the hotel. Uncle Nigel complained about the service and Sara asked him to keep his voice down because everyone was listening. I thought they were going to argue again but fortunately he was in a good mood. He was wearing a white polo shirt, showing off his arms. He says that he's got a good foundation for his tan. I've noticed that whenever he passes a mirror he stops and looks at himself in it. He's obviously pleased although if you ask me, he's looking rather red.

He says that tomorrow he's going to move down to Factor 9.

August 16th
Uncle Nigel has burnt himself.

He didn't say as much but it's pretty obvious. We had lunch in a café on the beach and I could see that his skin was an angry red around his neck and in the fleshy part of his legs. He also winced slightly when he sat down, so his back is probably bad too. Sara said she'd go into Bridgetown and buy some calamine lotion for him but he told her that he was perfectly all right and didn't need it.

But he did say he'd move back on to Factor 15.

It's very strange this business of the tan. I don't quite understand what Uncle Nigel is trying to prove. Sara told me (while he was in the toilet) that it's the same every year. Whenever he goes on holiday he smothers himself in oil and lies rigidly out in the open sun but he never has much success. I suppose his obsession must have something to do with his age. A lot of parents are the same. They get into their forties and off they go to the gym three times a week, pushing and pedalling and punishing themselves as they try to put a bit of shape back into their sagging bodies. Uncle Nigel's body is beyond hope as far as muscles are concerned. But at least he can give himself a bit of colour. He wants to go back to school bronzed and healthy. Perhaps for one term they'll stop calling him Porridge.

They didn't let me hire a jet ski even though it's my own money. Mum and Dad gave me a hundred pounds to spend. So Cassian and I went for a walk and then played football with some local kids we met. Before we left, I saw Nigel, stretched out in his usual place. He was reading *A Tale of Two Cities* by Charles Dickens but the oil and sweat were dripping off his fingers and blotching the pages. He also had the sun in his eyes and was having to squint horribly to read the words. But he won't wear sunglasses. He doesn't want them to spoil his tan.

Got back to the hotel at six o'clock. Uncle Nigel was having a shower by the pool. I could see that he'd fallen asleep in the sun. He was very red. At the same time, he must have left the Dickens novel leaning against him when he dropped off because there was a great rectangle on his stomach – the same size as a paperback book – which was as white as ever. The sun lounger had also made a wickerwork pattern on his back.

I waved to him and asked him how he was. He said he had a headache. He also had a heat blister on one cheek.

August 17th

Cassian's parents took me out for the day. We drove in an open-top jeep through the centre of the island. Lots of sugar cane and old plantation houses that make you think of pirates and slaves. We visited a cave. We had to wear plastic hats for protection and a tram took us deep down into the ground, through amazing caverns with petrified waterfalls, stalagmites and stalactites. I can never remember which is which. Cassian's dad is a writer. His mum is some sort of TV producer. The two of them didn't argue, which made a change.

I was sort of dreading getting back to the hotel,

wondering about N & S. No surprises there. He was still out on his sun lounger and Sara was sitting next to him, reminding him to turn over every half hour...like a chicken on a spit. She told me that he had decided he would be all right with Factor 9 again but I wouldn't have agreed. His shoulders were badly burned and there were two more blisters on his nose.

She rubbed in some more oil for him. I was surprised how horrible it smelled. It's yellow and it oozes out of the bottle, rippling between her fingers as she rubs it in. Disgusting.

I've caught the sun a bit myself but I'm being careful. I wear a T-shirt with wide sleeves and a Bart Simpson baseball cap. I've got my own sun cream too. If you ask me, Uncle Nigel is out of his mind. Hasn't he heard of skin cancer?

August 19th
He's got a tan! It's not exactly a Mr Universe shade of bronze but he's definitely brown from head to toe. There are one or two areas where the skin is still a bit red, under his arms and on the very top of his

head, but he says they'll soon blend in with the rest of him. He was in a really good mood this afternoon and even said that perhaps I can go on a jet ski after all.

It rained for the first time this afternoon. The rain out here is strange. One moment it's blazing sunlight and the next it's just bucketing down and everyone has to run for cover. But it's not like English rain. The water is softer. It's like standing in a warm shower. And it's over as quickly as it started, as if someone threw a switch.

Sara took me on the bus to Bridgetown, leaving Nigel on the beach (Factor 4). We walked round the port which was a jumble of sailing boats and huge, fat cruisers. She looked into chartering a boat for the day but when she found out the price she soon forgot that idea. Nigel would never agree to pay, she said, and at the same time she sort of sighed. So I asked her something I'd always wondered. 'Why did you marry Uncle Nigel?' I asked. 'Oh,' she said. 'He was very different when he was young. And so was I. I thought we'd be happy together.'

We went to a bar down on the dock. Sara bought

me an ice cream. For herself she ordered a large rum punch even though it was only half past three in the afternoon. She made me promise not to tell Uncle Nigel.

August 21st
Bad news. Uncle Nigel has completely peeled. So now he's back to square one.

August 22nd
Uncle Nigel spent the entire day (eight hours) on the beach but it looks as if his new skin is refusing to tan. He has moved down to sun protection Factor 2.

He and Sara had an unpleasant argument yesterday…the day he lost his tan. Apparently, when they woke up, the sheets were covered with bits of brown. At first Sara thought it was mould or something that had flaked off the ceiling. But it was actually dead skin. She said it made her feel sick and Nigel just flew at her. You could hear their voices down the corridor.

I saw Nigel stripping off on the beach. There was a

bright pink strip going from his neck to his belly as if someone had been trying to unwrap him in a hurry. This was where the old skin had fallen away. But new skin had already grown to take its place. As for the rest of his tanned skin, it was obvious that he was going to lose that too. It was already muddy and unhealthy. He couldn't move without a bit flaking off. He was doing what he could to save it. I noticed that he'd brought down a big bottle of After Sun and he was rubbing that in as if he thought it would somehow stick him back together again. I didn't think it would work.

I went out again with Cassian and also with his older brother, Nick. I told them about Uncle Nigel and they both thought it was very funny. Nick told me that in Victorian times nobody wanted to have a sun tan. It was considered socially inferior. This is something he learned at school.

When I got back to the hotel, Uncle Nigel was still lying there with Aunt Sara just a few metres away, sitting with her Stephen King under an umbrella. The book must have been amusing her because there was a definite smile on her face.

As for my uncle, I think the whole situation is getting out of hand. His new skin isn't tanning. But it is burning. It's already gone a virulent shade of crimson. Unlike me, he hasn't been wearing a hat and a large heat bubble has formed in the middle of his head. It's like one of those white blobs you get in cartoons when Jerry hits Tom with a hammer. All the other hotel guests have begun to avoid him. You can see, when they walk down to the sea. They make a circle so they don't have to get too close.

I notice, incidentally, that he's still reading *A Tale of Two Cities*. But we've been here now for almost two weeks and he's still only on page twelve.

August 25th

Cassian and Nick left today and the hotel feels empty without them. Another family arrived…three girls! To be honest, I'm beginning to look forward to going home. No news from Mum. She still hasn't had the baby. I'm missing her. And I'm really worried about Uncle Nigel.

All his old skin has gone now. It's either fallen off

or it's been taken over by the new skin which is a sort of mottled mauve and has a life of its own. His whole body is covered in boils like tiny volcanoes. These actually burst in the hot sun...I swear I'm not making it up. They burst and yellow pus oozes out. You can actually see it. Every ten minutes he seems to have another boil somewhere on his skin. There are also lots more sores on his face. They run down the side of his cheeks and onto his neck. If he had a chin I'm sure that would be covered in sores too.

And he's still trying to get a tan! This afternoon I'd had enough. I don't often talk to Uncle Nigel. For some reason I always seem to irritate him. But I did try telling him that he looked, frankly, horrible, and that I was really worried about him. I should have saved my breath! He almost chewed my head off, using the sort of language you wouldn't expect to hear coming from a head teacher. So then I tried to tell Aunt Sara what I thought.

ME: Aunt Sara, aren't you going to do something?

SARA: What do you mean?

ME: Uncle Nigel! He looks awful…

SARA: (with a sigh) What can I do, Tim? I'm afraid your uncle has never listened to me. Not ever. And he's been determined to get this tan.

ME: But he's killing himself.

SARA: I think you're exaggerating, dear. He'll be fine.

But he isn't fine. Dinner tonight was the most embarrassing night of my life.

We went to a posh restaurant. It should have been beautiful. The tables were outdoors, spread over two terraces. We sat with paper lanterns hanging over us and the silver waves almost lapping at our feet. Nigel walked very stiffly, like a robot. You could tell that his clothes were rubbing against his damaged skin and to him they must have felt like sandpaper.

He didn't make much sense over dinner. He ranted on about a boy called Charlie Meyer who obviously went to his school and who, equally obviously, was no favourite of his. He was still using a lot of four-letter words and I could see the other diners glancing round. One of the waiters came to see what the matter was and suddenly Uncle Nigel was violently sick! All over himself!

We left at once. Uncle Nigel groaned as we bundled him into a taxi. I could feel his skin under his shirt. It was damp and slimy. Aunt Sara didn't say anything until we got back to the hotel. Then... 'You can order from room service, Tim. And you'll have to put yourself to bed.'

'What about Uncle Nigel?'

'I'll look after him!'

August 27th

Uncle Nigel is no longer able to talk. Even if he could construct a sentence anyone could understand, he would be unable to say it as he has now managed to burn his lips so badly that they've gone black and shrivelled up. What was left of his hair has fallen out and his new skin has shrunk and torn so that you can actually see areas of his skull. I think he has also gone blind in one eye.

The hotel manager, Mr Jenson, has banned him from the beach as the other guests had finally complained. Mr Jenson had a meeting with my aunt and me. He said that in his opinion my uncle shouldn't be sunbathing any more.

JENSON: Forgive me, Mrs Howard. But I think this is a very unhealthy situation…

SARA: I have tried to stop him, Mr Jenson. This morning I even locked him in the bathroom. But he managed to force the window and climb down the drainpipe.

JENSON: Perhaps we should call for a doctor?

SARA: I'm sure that's not necessary…

She said she'd been trying to stop him but I'm not sure that's true. She was still rubbing oil into him every morning and evening. I'd seen her. But I didn't say anything.

I am beginning to feel very uneasy about all this.

August 28th

Yesterday evening, Uncle Nigel ran away.

He had another argument with Aunt Sara. I heard vague, muffled shouts and then the slamming of the door. When I looked out of the window – the sun was just beginning to set – I saw him race out of the hotel, staggering towards the beach. He could hardly stand up straight. He was wearing shorts and nothing else and he was completely unrecognisable. He had no skin at all. His eyes bulged out of his skull and his lips had shrunk back to reveal not just his teeth but his gums. Every step he took, he moaned. At one point he staggered and fell back against the hotel wall. One of the guests saw him and actually screamed.

This morning he was gone. But he had left a bloody imprint of himself on the wall.

August 30th

I can't help but feel that Aunt Sara is completely different. There has been no news of Uncle Nigel and he hasn't been seen for two days but she hasn't been worried. She has been drinking a lot of rum. Last night she got drunk and ended up dancing with one of the waiters.

I can't wait to get home. I spoke to Mum this morning. It seems I have a baby sister. They're going to call her Lucy.

Mum asked me about the holiday. I told her about the island and about the family I met but I decided not to say anything about Uncle Nigel.

August 31st

Uncle Nigel is dead!

Some fishermen found him yesterday, lying flat on the beach. At first they thought he must have been eaten up and spat out by sharks. His whole body was a mass of oozing sores, gashes and poisoned flesh. He no longer had any eyes. What had happened was that he had fallen asleep again in the sun. And this time he hadn't woken up.

They were only able to recognise him by his Marks and Spencer shorts.

Aunt Sara didn't even sound surprised when they told her. She just said 'Oh.'

And I thought I saw her smile.

September 2nd
Back in England. Thank goodness.

Mum and Dad were meant to meet me at Heathrow Airport but as it turned out there was one last, nasty surprise waiting for me when we finally landed. It turned out that my new sister, Lucy, had caught some sort of virus. It wasn't anything very serious – just one of the things that newly-born babies often get – but she'd had to go back into hospital for the night and Mum and Dad were with her. Sara's name was called out over the intercom and we lugged our cases over to the information desk where we were given the news. I'd have to stay at her house – just for the night. Mum and Dad would come and pick me up in the morning.

So it was back to Fulham and the Victorian terrace. I have to say that I walked in with a certain feeling of dread. It was Sara's house now, of course. But it had once been Nigel's and I could still feel him in there. It wasn't just his ghost. In a way it was worse than that.

The drab wallpaper and the shelves stuffed with fat, serious books. The old-fashioned furniture, the heavy curtains blotting out the light, the smell of damp. It was as if his spirit was everywhere. He was dead. But while we were in the house, his memory lived on.

Aunt Sara must have felt it too. Before she'd even unpacked, she rang an estate agent and told him that she wanted to put the house on the market immediately. She said she planned to emigrate to Florida.

We had supper together – take-away Chinese – but neither of us ate very much and we hardly talked at all. She wanted to be on her own. I could tell. In a funny way, she seemed almost suspicious of me. I noticed her glancing at me once or twice as if she was worried about something. It was as if she was waiting for me to blame her for Nigel's death. But it hadn't been her fault. She hadn't done anything wrong.

Had she?

I went to bed early that night. In the spare room. But I couldn't sleep.

I found myself thinking about everything that had happened. Over and over again the pieces went through my mind until a picture began to form. I rolled over and tried to think of something else. But I couldn't. Because what I was seeing now, what I should have seen all along, was so horribly obvious.

'*I have plans...*'

That's what Sara had told my mum before we left for the holiday. She hadn't wanted me to come from the very start. It was almost as if she had known what was going to happen and hadn't wanted me to be there, as a witness. She hadn't made Uncle Nigel lie in the sun, but now I thought about it, she had never actually discouraged him either. And his death hadn't upset her at all. She'd been drinking rum and dancing with the waiters before they'd even discovered the corpse.

No! It was crazy! After all, she *had* packed all those bottles, the different sun-tan lotions. She'd even rubbed them in for him. As I lay in the darkness, I remembered the yellow ooze spilling out of the bottle, rippling through her fingers as she massaged his back.

Once again I smelled it – thick and greasy – and at the same time I remembered something Nigel had said just after we'd arrived. He'd been examining one of the bottles and he'd said:

'*Have you opened this?*'

Maybe that was what made me get up. I couldn't sleep anyway so I got up and went downstairs. I don't know why I tiptoed but I did. And there was Aunt Sara, standing in the kitchen, humming to herself.

She was surrounded by bottles. I recognised them at once. Factor 15, Factor 9 and Factor 4. The water-resistant oil, the hypo-allergenic oil and all the other oil. The Before Sun and the After Sun protection. She was emptying them, one at a time, into a large green tin. And no matter what it said on the labels, it was the same gold-coloured oil that poured into the tin and I guessed that this was where the oil had really come from in the first place.

QUIKCOOK VEGETABLE OIL – FOR FASTER FRYING

Big red letters on the side of the tin. My aunt

continued emptying the bottles, getting rid of the evidence. I crept back to bed and counted the hours until my parents finally came.

the
MONKEY'S
ear

The story began,
as so many stories
do, in the *souk* –
or covered
market – of
Marrakesh.

It has been said that there are as many stories in the *souk* as there are products and if you have ever lost yourself in the dozens of covered walkways jammed on all sides with the hundreds of shops and little stalls groaning under the weight of thousands of objects from trinkets and spice bottles to carpets and coffee beans, you will realise that this must add up to more stories than could be told in a hundred-and-one nights or even a hundred-and-one years.

The Beckers had come to Morocco on holiday and had found themselves in the *souk* of Marrakesh only because they had accepted a free tour to go there. All the hotels offered free tours. The idea, of course, was to get the tourists to spend their money once they get to the market. But it wasn't going to work this time...not with the Beckers.

'It's too hot here,' Brenda Becker was complaining. 'And all these flies! We shouldn't have come! I said I didn't want to come. And anyway it's not as if there's anything to buy. All this foreign muck...' She swatted at a fly buzzing around her plump, rather sunburned face. 'Why can't we just find a branch of Marks and Spencer?' she moaned.

Her husband, Brian Becker, gritted his teeth and followed behind her. It seemed to him that he was always one step behind her, like Prince Philip and the flipping Queen. It was certainly true that she ruled over everything he did. That was why he enjoyed his job so much – he worked as a traffic warden. First of all, it got him away from her. But also it meant that, at least when he was out on the road, he was in charge.

A salesman in torn jeans and a grubby T-shirt came up to him, showing off a string of beads. Brian waved a tired hand. 'Go away!' he shouted. 'Sod off, Sinbad!' He stopped and wiped the sweat off his forehead, where it had dripped through what was left of his hair. Brian Becker was a small, weedy man with a thin face and slightly orange skin. He had lost his hair before he was twenty and even now he was embarrassed by the sight of his head, bald and speckled like an egg. That was another good thing about being a traffic warden. He liked the uniform. It made him feel smart, particularly the cap which disguised his baldness. He often wore the cap at home, in bed and even in the bath. But dressed as he was now, in shorts that were much too wide for his spindly legs and a brilliant shirt festooned with flowers (Brenda had chosen it for him before they left) he looked simply ridiculous.

A twelve-year-old boy, walking just beside Arthur, completed the family. This was Bart Becker, their only child. Bart had been fortunate in that he had inherited neither his father's looks nor his mother's excessive weight. He was slim with a pale face and fair hair that rose over his forehead rather like his favourite comic-book hero, Tintin. He was the only one of the three who was enjoying his time in the *souk*. The jumble of colours, the rich smells and the shouts of the traders woven in with the distant wail of pipes and drums all seemed mysterious and exciting to him. Perhaps the main difference between Bart and his parents was that from a very early age he had enjoyed reading books. He loved stories and to him life was a constant adventure. To his parents it was simply something they had to get through.

'We're lost!' Brenda exclaimed. 'This is all your fault, Brian. I want to go back to the hotel.'

'All right! All right!' Brian licked his lips and looked around him. The trouble was that here, in the middle of the *souk*, every passageway looked much like the next one and he had long ago lost any sense of direction. 'It's that way,' he said, pointing.

'We just came from there!'

'Did we?'

'You're an idiot, Brian. My mother always said it and I should have listened to her. We're lost and we're never going to get out of this wretched place.'

'All right! All right!' Brian was forever repeating the same two words. 'I'll ask someone.'

There was a shop to one side selling antique daggers and pieces of jewellery. As Brenda had already pointed out – several times – everything in the *souk* was probably fake. Most of it was no more antique than her own artificial hip. But this stall was different. The knives looked somehow a little more deadly and the jewels glowed just a little more brightly. And there was something else. The very building itself, dark and crooked, seemed older than the rest of the *souk*, as if it had been there first and the rest of the market had slowly grown around it.

They went in. As they passed through the door all the sounds of the *souk* were abruptly shut off. They found themselves standing on a thick carpet in a cave-like room with the smell of sweet mint tea hanging in the air.

'There's nobody here!' Brenda exclaimed.

'Look at this! This is wicked!' Bart had found a long, curving sword. The hilt was encrusted with dark green stones and the blade was stained with what could have been dried blood.

'Don't touch it, Bart!' Brenda snapped. 'It's dirty.'

'And we'll have to pay for it if you break it,' Brian added.

A curtain hanging over a door rippled and a young

boy appeared. He must have been about the same age as Bart but he was shorter with very dark skin, black hair and a round, slightly feminine face. He would have been handsome but for the fact that one of his eyes had a large sty, forcing it into a squint, and this made him look almost sinister.

'Good morning. You want buy?' His English was heavily accented and sing-song. He had probably learnt it parrot-fashion from his parents.

'We're not here to buy, thank you very much,' Brenda said.

'We're looking for the way out. The exit.' Brian jerked his thumb in the direction of the door. 'Go to the hotel. Taxi!'

'We have fine jewellery,' the boy replied. 'Nice necklace for lady. Or maybe you like carpet?'

'We don't want jewellery or carpets,' Brian replied angrily. 'We want to go home!'

'This is useless, Brian!' Brenda muttered.

'I sell you something very special!' The boy looked around him and his eyes settled on a wrinkled object lying on a shelf. It was brown and curved, half wrapped in mouldy tissue paper. 'I sell you this!' He took it and placed it on the counter.

'We don't want it,' Brian said.

'It's revolting,' Brenda agreed.

'What is it?' Bart asked.

The boy leered. 'It is my uncle's,' he said. 'The monkey's ear. It is very old. Very powerful. Very secret.'

'What does it do?' Bart asked.

'Don't encourage him, Bart,' his mother said.

But it was too late. The boy ignored her. 'The monkey's ear gives four wishes,' he said. He counted on his fingers as if checking his English. 'One. Two. Three. Four. You say to the ear what you want and you get. Very rare! But also very cheap! I give you good price...'

'We don't want it,' Brenda insisted.

Bart reached out and took it. The ear nestled in the palm of his hand. It seemed to be made of leather but there were a few hairs on the back. The inside of the ear was black and felt like plastic. He rather hoped it was plastic. He didn't particularly want to imagine that he was holding a real ear, severed from a real monkey.

'Four wishes,' the boy repeated. 'One. Two. Three. Four.'

'Let's get out of here,' Brenda said.

'No. I want it!' Bart looked up at his parents. 'You said I could have something from the *souk* and I want this!'

'But why?' A trickle of sweat dripped off Brian's chin and he wiped it with the cuff of his shirt. 'What do you want it for?'

'I just want it. I think it's cool...'

'Brian...?' Brenda began, using her special tone of voice. She always used it when she was about to explode.

'How much do you want for it?' Brian asked.

'A thousand dirhem,' the boy replied.

'A thousand dirhem? That's...That's...' Brian tried to work it out.

'It's too much,' Brenda cut in. 'It's more than fifty pounds.'

'Will you take five hundred dirhem?' Bart asked.

'Seven hundred,' the boy replied.

'Come on, Bart.' Brian grabbed hold of his son's arm. 'We didn't come in to buy anything. We just wanted to find the way out!'

'Six hundred!' Bart insisted. He wasn't quite sure why he wanted the monkey's ear but now that he had decided on it he was determined to have his way.

'Yes. Is deal. Six hundred.' The boy rapidly folded the monkey's ear in its dirty wrapping and held it out.

Brian grimaced, then counted out the notes. 'That's still twenty quid,' he complained. 'It seems a lot to pay for a bit of rubbish...'

'You promised,' Bart said. He'd actually worked out that the price was nearer thirty pounds but thought it better not to say.

They left the shop and within minutes they had once again disappeared into the swirl of the *souk*. Back in the shop, the curtain had moved for a second time and an enormously fat man had come in, dressed in traditional white robes that reached down to his sandals. The man had popped out to buy some

Turkish Delight and was licking the last traces from his fingers as he sat down behind the counter. He glanced at the boy who was still counting the money. The man frowned and the two of them began to talk in their own language so that even if the Beckers had been there they wouldn't have understood a word that was said.

'Some tourists came in, Uncle. Stupid English tourists. They gave me six hundred dirhem!'

'What did you sell them?'

'The monkey's ear.'

The man's eyes widened. He stood up quickly and went over to the shelf. One look told him all he needed to know. *'You sold them the monkey's ear!'* he exclaimed. *'Where are they? Where did they go?'* He grabbed hold of the boy and drew him closer. *'Tell me!'*

'They've left! I thought you'd be pleased, Uncle! You told me that the monkey's ear was worthless. You said it was...'

'I said we couldn't sell it! We mustn't sell it! The monkey that the ear was taken from was sick. You

*have no idea of the danger! Quickly, you son-of-a-
goat! You must find the tourists. You must give them
back their money. You must get it back...'*

`But you said...!'

*`Find them! Go now! In the name of Allah, let's pray
it's not too late!'* The man pushed the boy out of the
shop. *`Search everywhere!'*

The boy ran out into the *souk*. The man sank back
into his seat, his head buried in his hands.

It was already too late. The Beckers had managed
to find their way out and were by now in a taxi on the
way back to their hotel. And two days later they left
Marrakesh. The monkey's ear went with them.

The Beckers lived in a modern bungalow in Stanmore,
a sprawling suburb to the north of London. They had
been home for a week when Brenda stumbled on the
monkey's ear. She was cleaning Bart's bedroom.
Brenda had a strange way of cleaning. Somehow it
always involved searching every drawer and
cupboard, reading Bart's diary and letters and

generally poking around wherever she could. She was the sort of mother who always believed the worst of her child. She was sure he kept secrets from her. Perhaps he had started smoking. Or perhaps he was gay. Whatever he was hiding, she was determined to be the first to find out.

As usual though, she had found nothing. She had come upon the monkey's ear underneath a pile of Tintin comics and she carried it downstairs in order to prove a point.

Bart had just got home from school. Brian had also got back from work. He'd had a disappointing day. Although he'd been out in the street for nine hours, he'd only issued three hundred and seven parking tickets, far short of his record. He was sitting in the kitchen, still wearing his uniform and precious cap, eating a fish-finger sandwich. Bart was also at the table, doing his homework.

'I see you've still got this filthy thing,' Brenda exclaimed.

'Mum...' Bart began. He knew his mother must have been looking through his room.

'We paid all that money for it and you've just shoved it in a drawer.' She sniffed indignantly. 'It's a complete waste. We should never have bought it.'

'It's not true,' Bart protested. 'I took it to school and showed everyone. They thought it was creepy.'

'Have you made any wishes?' Brian giggled. 'You could wish yourself top of the class. It would make a pleasant change.'

'No.' Bart had almost forgotten what the boy with the sty had said but the truth was that he would have been too embarrassed to make a wish using the monkey's ear. It would be like saying he believed in fairies or Santa Claus. He had wanted the ear because it was strange and ugly. Not because he thought it could make him rich.

His father must have been reading his mind. 'It's all just rubbish,' he said. 'A monkey's ear that gives you wishes! That's just a load of cobblers!'

'That's not true!' Bart couldn't stop himself arguing with his father. He did it all the time. 'We had a story in school this week. It was exactly the same...except it wasn't a monkey's ear. It was a monkey's paw. And it wasn't as good as an ear because it only gave you three wishes, not four.'

'So what happened in the story?' Brian asked.

'We haven't finished it yet.' This wasn't actually true. Their English teacher had finished the story – which had been written by someone called Edgar Allan Poe – but it had been a hot day and Bart had been day-dreaming so he hadn't heard the end.

Brian took the ear from his wife and turned it over in his hand. He wrinkled his nose. The ear was soft and hairy and felt warm to the touch. 'It would be bloody marvellous if it worked,' he said.

'What would you wish for, Dad?' Bart asked.

Brian held the ear up between his finger and thumb. He raised his other hand for silence. 'I wish for a Rolls-Royce!' he exclaimed.

'What a lot of nonsense!' his wife muttered.

The doorbell rang.

Brian stared at Brenda. Brenda sniffed. 'I'll get it,' Bart said.

He went to the door and opened it. Of course there wasn't going to be a Rolls-Royce there. He didn't expect that for a minute. Even so, he was a little disappointed to discover that he was right, that the street was empty apart from a small, Japanese man holding a brown paper bag.

'Yes?' Bart said.

'This is 15 Green Lane?'

'Yes.' That was their address.

The Japanese man held up the paper bag. 'This is the take-away you ordered.'

'We didn't order any take-away...'

Brenda had come into the hall behind Bart. 'Who is it?' she asked.

'It's someone saying we ordered take-away,' Bart told her.

Brenda glanced at the Japanese man with distaste. She didn't like foreign food and, for that matter, she didn't like foreigners either. 'You've got the wrong house,' she said. 'We don't want any of that here.'

'15 Green Lane,' the Japanese man insisted. 'Sushi for three people.'

'Sushi?'

'It's all paid for.' The man thrust the bag into Bart's

hand and before anyone could say anything he had turned and walked away.

Bart carried the bag into the kitchen. 'What is it?' his father asked.

'It's a Japanese take-away,' Bart said. 'He said it was sushi…'

Brian frowned. 'There isn't a Japanese take-away around here.'

'He said it was already paid for,' Brenda said.

'Well, we might as well have it then.'

None of the Beckers had ever eaten sushi before. When they opened the bag they found a plastic box containing three sets of chopsticks and twelve neat rolls of rice stuffed with crab meat and cucumber. Brian picked up one of the pieces with his fingers and ate it. 'Disgusting!' he announced.

'I'll give it to the cat,' Brenda said.

Brian sighed. 'Just for a minute there, I thought that stupid monkey's ear had actually worked,' he said. 'I thought you'd open the door and find I'd won a brand-new Rolls-Royce in a competition or something. Wouldn't that have been great!'

'A Rolls-Royce would be a stupid wish anyway,' Brenda said. 'We could never afford to run it. Just think of the insurance!'

'What would you wish for, Mum?' Bart asked.

'I don't know...' Brenda thought for a minute. 'I'd probably wish for a million pounds. I'd wish I could win the lottery.'

'All right then!' Brian held up the monkey's paw for a second time. 'I wish for a ton of money!'

But nothing happened. The door-bell didn't ring. Nor did the telephone. When the lottery was drawn later that evening (it was a Wednesday) Brian hadn't even got one number right. He went to bed as poor and as frustrated as he had been when he woke up.

There was, however, one strange event the next day. Brian was out on his rounds and had just given a parking ticket to an old-age pensioner and was on his way down to the station where he knew he would find at least a dozen illegally parked cars when he came upon a woman leaning under the bonnet of a small white van. Brian smiled to himself. The van had stopped on a yellow line. He reached for his ticket machine.

'You can't park there!' he exclaimed in his usual way.

The woman straightened up and closed the bonnet. She was young and rather pretty – younger and prettier, certainly, than Brenda. 'I'm very sorry,' she said. 'My van broke down. I'm just on my way to the market. But I've managed to fix it. You're not going to give me a ticket, are you?'

'Well...' Brian pretended to think about it but in fact he had no real reason to ticket her, not if she was about to move. 'All right,' he said. 'I'll let you off this time.'

'You're very kind.' The woman reached into the van and took a small tin off the front seat. The tin had a yellow and black label with the words ELM CROSS FARM printed on the front. 'Let me give you this,' she said. 'To thank you.'

'What is it?' Brian wasn't supposed to accept gifts but he was intrigued.

'It's what I sell at the market,' the woman

explained. 'I have a small farm in Hertfordshire. I keep bees. And this is our best honey. It's really delicious. I hope you enjoy it.'

'Well, I don't know...' Brian began. But the woman had already got back into the van and a moment later she drove off.

The honey was delicious. Brian and Bart ate it for tea that evening although Brenda, who was on a diet, refused. She was in a bad mood. The washing machine had broken that afternoon and the repair man had said it would cost ninety pounds to mend. 'I don't know where I'm going to find the cash,' she said. Her eye fell on the monkey's ear that was still lying on the side where they had left it the night before. 'I notice we didn't get a single penny from that stupid thing,' she said. 'If only it did have the power to grant wishes. I'd have a new washing machine for a start. And a new house. And a new husband too, for that matter...'

'What's wrong with me?' Brian complained.

'Well, you haven't got much of a job. You don't earn enough. You pick your nose in bed. And I always think it's a shame you lost your hair. You looked much more handsome when you were younger.'

It was a particularly nasty thing to say. Brenda knew that Brian was sensitive about his appearance but whenever she was in a bad mood she always took it out on him.

Brian scowled. He snatched up the monkey's ear. 'I wish I had my hair again,' he cried.

'You're wasting your time,' Brenda muttered. 'You're bald now and you'll be bald until you die. In fact that ear's got more hair on it than you have!'

That night the weather changed. Although it had been a beautiful day, by the time the Beckers went to bed the clouds had rolled in and the wind had risen and just before midnight there was a sudden, deafening rumble of thunder. Brenda was jerked out of her sleep. 'What was that?' she whimpered.

There was a second boom of thunder. At the same time, the clouds opened and a torrent of rain crashed down, rattling on the roof and driving into the windows with such force that the glass shivered in the frames. The wind became stronger. The trees along

Green Lane bent and twisted, then jerked crazily as whole branches were torn off and thrown across the street. Lightning flickered in the air. Somewhere a burglar alarm went off. Dogs howled and barked. The wind screamed and the rain hammered into the house like machine-gun bullets.

'What's going on?' Brenda cried.

Brian went over to the window in his pyjamas but he could hardly see anything. The rain was lashing at the glass, a solid curtain that seemed to enshroud the bungalow. 'It's gone crazy!' he exclaimed.

'But the weather forecast didn't say anything about rain!'

'The weather forecast was wrong!' There was an explosion above Brian's head and something red and solid hurtled past, disintegrating on the front drive.

'What was that?'

'It's the bloody chimney! The whole place is coming down!'

In fact the bungalow stood up to the storm but the following morning at breakfast, the Beckers realised that they were going to have to pay for more than a new washing machine. The storm had torn off the chimney and part of the roof. Brian's car had been blown over on to its side. His rockery was missing. All the fish had been sucked out of his fish-pond and his garden fence was somewhere on the other side of London.

Curiously, theirs was the only house that seemed to have been damaged. It was as if the storm had descended on them and them alone.

'I just don't understand it!' Brenda wailed. 'What's going on? Why us? What have we done to deserve this?'

'It was a blooming hurricane!' Brian said. 'A hurricane! That's what it was!'

Bart had been listening to his parents in silence but Brian's last words somehow reminded him of something. A hurricane? He thought back – to tea the day before, and breakfast before that. He looked at the monkey's ear, lying on the sideboard. His father had made three wishes and nothing had happened.

Or had it?

'It worked!' he muttered. 'The monkey's ear...'

'What are you talking about?' his father demanded.

'It worked, Dad! At least, it worked – sort of. But...' It took Bart a few moments to collect his thoughts. But he knew he was right. He had to be.

'The monkey's ear didn't give us anything,' Brenda said.

'But it did, Mum.' Bart reached out and took it. 'We made three wishes and we got three things – only they weren't the right things. It's as if it didn't hear us properly. Maybe that's why it was so cheap.'

'Twenty quid isn't cheap,' Brian sniffed.

'No, Dad. But if the monkey's ear had been working properly, it would have been a bargain.'

'What are you going on about?'

Bart paused. 'What was your first wish?' he asked.

'I wanted a ton of money.'

'No.' Bart shook his head. 'Your first wish was a Rolls-Royce. And what happened? There was that funny Japanese man at the door and he gave you...'

'He gave us some horrible sushi,' Brenda interrupted.

'Yes. But what are sushi? They're rolls of rice! Don't you see? The ear didn't hear you properly. You asked for a Rolls-Royce and it gave you some rolls of rice!'

'The second wish was a ton of money,' Brenda said.

'That's right. And then you met that woman and she gave you a tin of honey. It was almost the same but it got it wrong a second time. And then, last night...'

'I said I wanted my hair again,' Brian remembered.

'Yes. And what did we get instead?' Brian and Brenda stared at Bart. 'We got a hurricane!'

There was a long silence. All three of them were staring at the ear.

'It's a deaf monkey!' Brian shouted.

'Yes.'

'Blooming heck!' He licked his lips. 'But in that case, if only I'd spoken a little louder...I could have had anything I wanted!'

Brenda's eyes widened. 'You've still got one wish left!' she exclaimed.

Bart snatched the ear. 'But it's my monkey's ear!'

he said. 'You bought it for me and this time I want to make the wish. I can get a new bike. I can never have to go back to school. I can be a millionaire. I want to make the wish!'

'Forget it!' Brian's hand flew out and grabbed hold of the ear. 'We've only got one more chance. I'm head of this family...'

'Dad...!'

'Give it to me!'

'No!'

Father and son were both fighting for the ear while Brenda looked on, still trying to make sense of it all.

'I want it, Dad!' Bart yelled.

'I wish you'd go to hell!'

The words were no sooner out of Brian's mouth than there was a flash and an explosion accompanied by a cloud of green smoke. When Brian and Brenda next opened their eyes, the monkey's ear was lying on the kitchen table. There was no sign of Bart.

Brenda was the first to recover. 'You idiot!' she screeched. 'You nincompoop! What did you say?'

'What did I say...?' Brian remembered his words and his face went pale.

'You told him to go to hell!' She sat down, her mouth dropping open. 'Our son! Our only boy! That was what you wished!'

'Wait a minute! Wait a minute!' Brian thought feverishly. 'You heard what he said! The monkey's ear is broken. It doesn't hear properly.'

'You told him to go to hell!'

Since then, Brian and Brenda Becker have looked for Bart on a hill and in a well. Recently, they moved to the city of Hull and they're almost certain that one day he'll turn up there.

But they haven't found him yet.

the shortest
HORROR
story
ever written

I want
to tell you
how this story
got included
in this book.

About a week before the book was published, I broke into the offices of Orchard Books which are located in a rather grubby street near Liverpool Street Station. Maybe you haven't noticed but the book you are holding at this very minute was published by Orchard and I wanted to get my hands on it because, you see, I'd had an idea.

Generally speaking, publishers are stupid, lazy people. Orchard Books have about twenty people working for them but not one of them noticed that a window had been forced open in the middle of the night and that someone had added a couple of pages to the collection of horror stories that was sitting by the computer, waiting to be sent to the printers. I had brought these pages with me, you see, because I wanted to add my own message to the book. Nobody noticed and nobody cared and if you are reading this then I'm afraid my plan has worked and you are about to discover the meaning of true horror. Get ready – because here it comes.

Twelve years ago I desperately wanted to be a writer and so I wrote a horror story (based on my own experiences) which was rejected by every publisher in London because, they claimed, it wasn't frightening enough! Of course, none of them had the faintest idea what horror really meant because they had never actually committed a murder whereas I, my dear reader, had committed several.

My Uncle Frederick was my first victim, followed by my next-door neighbour (an unpleasant little man with a moustache and a smelly cat), two total strangers, an actor who once had a bit part in Eastenders and a Jehovah's Witness who happened to knock at my door while I was cooking lunch. Unfortunately, my adventures came to an end when a dim-witted policeman stopped my car just as I was disposing of the last body and I was arrested and sent to a lunatic asylum for life. Recently, however, I escaped and it was after that that I had the wonderful idea which you are reading about at this very moment and which can be summarised in three simple stages. Drop into the offices of one of those smarmy publishers in London and slip a couple of pages into somebody else's book (with many apologies to Anthony Horowitz, whoever he may be). Exit quietly and stay in hiding until the book is published. Return only when the book is in the shops and then wait in the background, until some poor fool buys it and follow that person home...

Yes, dear reader, at this very moment I could be sitting outside your home or your school or wherever you happen to be and if by any chance you are the one I've chosen, I'm afraid you're about to learn a lesson about horror that I know you'd prefer to miss. Orchard Books are also going to wish that they'd published me all those years ago, especially when they start losing readers in particularly nasty ways, one by one. Understanding will come – but I'm afraid you're going to have to read this whole story again.

Start at the beginning. Only this time look carefully at the first word of each sentence. Or to be more precise, the first letter of each first word. Now, at last, I hope you can see quite how gloriously, hideously mad I really am – although for you, perhaps, it may already be too late.

Enter the strange and twisted
world of Anthony Horowitz –
if you dare!

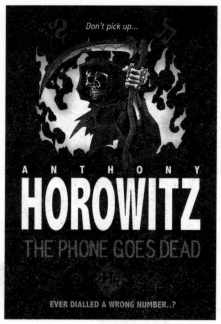

ISBN 978 1 84616 972 4   £3.99

Two twisted tales to curdle your blood.

David's mobile won't stop ringing, but these are no ordinary callers. He seems to have a hotline to heaven...or hell.

Isabel has a nasty feeling that the Victorian bath her parents have installed is *waiting* for her. But it won't be a bubble bath she gets, more of a bloodbath.

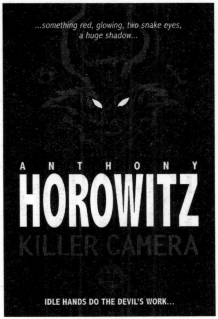

...something red, glowing, two snake eyes, a huge shadow...

ANTHONY
HOROWITZ
KILLER CAMERA

IDLE HANDS DO THE DEVIL'S WORK...

ISBN 978 1 84616 971 7   £3.99

Two spine-chilling stories guaranteed to keep you awake at night.

Jamie is pleased with the camera he finds at a car boot sale, until he realises that everything he photographs breaks...or dies.

Henry soon finds that his new computer has a life of its own, and it's not afraid to gamble – with people's lives!

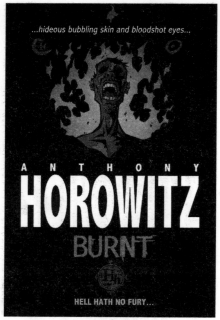

...hideous bubbling skin and bloodshot eyes...

A N T H O N Y
HOROWITZ
BURNT

HELL HATH NO FURY...

ISBN 978 1 84616 966 3   £3.99

Three ~~Two~~ creepy stories to send shivers down your spine.

Uncle Nigel is determined to get a sun tan. But Tim is sure there's something sinister going on as his uncle's skin starts to frazzle and his brain begins to fry.

When Bart buys a magical monkey's ear in a market in Marrakesh, he discovers that making wishes is a dangerous game.

'It's all around you. Alive. Waiting...'

ANTHONY
HOROWITZ
SCARED

IF YOU GO DOWN TO THE WOODS TODAY...

ISBN 978 1 84616 968 7   £3.99

Three sinister stories to fill you with fear.

Gary hates the countryside. It's boring. But something has got it in for Gary. Perhaps the countryside hates him too?

Kevin loves computer games, but this latest one breaks all the rules, and it's ruthless....

Howard's in heaven...so why does it feel more like hell?

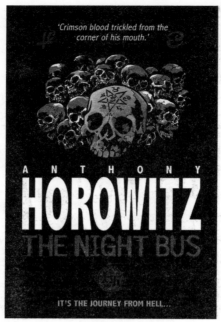

'Crimson blood trickled from the
corner of his mouth.'

ANTHONY HOROWITZ
THE NIGHT BUS

IT'S THE JOURNEY FROM HELL...

ISBN 978 1 84616 967 0   £3.99

Three terrifying tales you'll wish you'd never read.

It's Halloween but the living dead on the night bus home aren't trick-or-treaters!

When his dad picks up a hitchhiker, Jacob finds himself in a life-or-death situation. Someone is harbouring a deadly secret.

And who is the man with the yellow face in Peter's passport photo – because it isn't him, is it?